No Lex 11·12

HIAWATHA
Messenger of Peace

HIAWATHA
Messenger of Peace

DENNIS BRINDELL FRADIN

Illustrated with ten photographs in color
and ten in black and white

Margaret K. McElderry Books
New York

Maxwell Macmillan Canada · Toronto

Maxwell Macmillan International · New York Oxford Singapore Sydney

Margaret K. McElderry Books
Macmillan Publishing Company, 866 Third Avenue, New York, NY 10022

Maxwell Macmillan Canada, Inc.
1200 Eglinton Avenue East, Suite 200, Don Mills, Ontario M3C 3N1
Macmillan Publishing Company is part of the
Maxwell Communication Group of Companies.
First edition   Printed in the United States of America
10   9   8   7   6   5   4   3   2   1

Library of Congress Cataloging-in-Publication Data
Fradin, Dennis B.
Hiawatha : messenger of peace / by Dennis Brindell Fradin ; map by
Tom Dunnington. — 1st ed.   p.   cm.
Summary: Recounts the life of the fifteenth-century Iroquois
Indian who brought five tribes together to form the long-lasting
Iroquois Federation.
ISBN 0-689-50519-1
1. Hiawatha, 15th cent.—Juvenile literature.   2. Iroquois
Indians—Biography—Juvenile literature.   3. Iroquois Indians—
Juvenile literature.   [1. Hiawatha, 15th cent.   2. Iroquois
Indians—Biography.]   I. Title.
E99.I7H484   1991   973'.0497502—dc20
[B]   [92]   90-26312

For My Beautiful Sister,
*L*ORI *F*RADIN,
with Love

HIAWATHA
Messenger of Peace

HIAWATHA is one of the most familiar of American Indian names. There are Hiawatha parks, woods, and streets. In Michigan there is a huge statue that is supposed to portray Hiawatha. What few people realize is that generally the Hiawatha being honored never existed. There was a real Hiawatha, but only a small number of people know about him.

The American author Henry Schoolcraft began the confusion in the mid-1800s by writing *The Myth of Hiawatha*. This book of Indian legends tells of a hero who can take mile-long steps and also turn into a wolf. Schoolcraft wrongly named his hero *Hiawatha*. He was really Manabozho, a god of the Chippewa tribe, which lived near Lake Superior in Michigan, Minnesota, and Canada.

This statue in Ironwood, Michigan, is called
Hiawatha, the World's Tallest Indian,
but it is not of the real Hiawatha.

Henry Wadsworth Longfellow.

The poet Henry Wadsworth Longfellow read Schoolcraft's book and loved the sound of the name *Hiawatha*. Longfellow used the name for his hero in *The Song of Hiawatha,* a book-length poem published in 1855. Longfellow's Hiawatha is a young chief who can talk to animals and outrun an arrow shot through the air. He marries Minnehaha and has many adventures, but at the end he meets white people and decides to become a Christian. *The Song of Hiawatha* soon sold a million copies—a tremendous number for a poetry book—but there was an unfortunate result. Now, whenever the name *Hiawatha* is mentioned, most people think of Longfellow's character rather than of the flesh-and-blood man.

Although he couldn't take mile-long steps or outrun an arrow, the real Hiawatha was in many ways more remarkable than Schoolcraft's and Longfellow's heroes. The real Hiawatha was one of history's great peacemakers. Centuries ago he helped convince the five Iroquois tribes of what is now New York State to stop fighting each other and join as one people. Hiawatha then helped make laws for the Iroquois so that they would live in peace. Many historians feel that, through a chain of events, all Americans live by some of these laws today.

Thousands of years ago, the people who became known as the

The Death of Minnehaha, *by the famous American*
printmakers Currier & Ives, illustrates a scene from Longfellow's
The Song of Hiawatha.

OPPOSITE:
Map of present-day New York State,
showing where the five Iroquois tribes lived.

Iroquois Indians came to present-day New York State. Over time, they divided into five separate tribes that shared similar customs and languages. These tribes were the Mohawk, the Oneida, the Onondaga, the Cayuga, and the Seneca. Many of the Iroquois say that Hiawatha was born in an Onondaga village, but it is also claimed that he was born among the Mohawks.

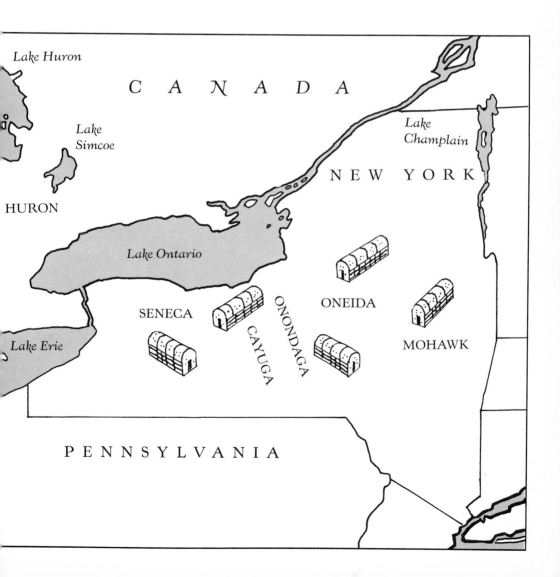

Iroquois longhouses. The one at left is incomplete.

Exactly when Hiawatha lived is also a mystery. Some Iroquois claim that he walked the earth a thousand years ago, yet most historians place him in the 1400s or 1500s. Several scholars who spoke to the Iroquois during the 1800s figured that Hiawatha lived in the mid-1400s, about fifty years before Christopher Columbus made his famous voyage to the New World in 1492. The name *Hiawatha* was given to him in later life. His childhood name is unknown, as are the details of his early years. But since we know a great deal about the Iroquois way of life, we can make educated guesses about Hiawatha's childhood.

Hiawatha almost certainly grew up in a longhouse—an oblong structure made of wooden poles and bark. Longhouses

The inside of an Iroquois longhouse. The woman is grinding corn. Earthenware items used by the Iroquois in daily life can also be seen.

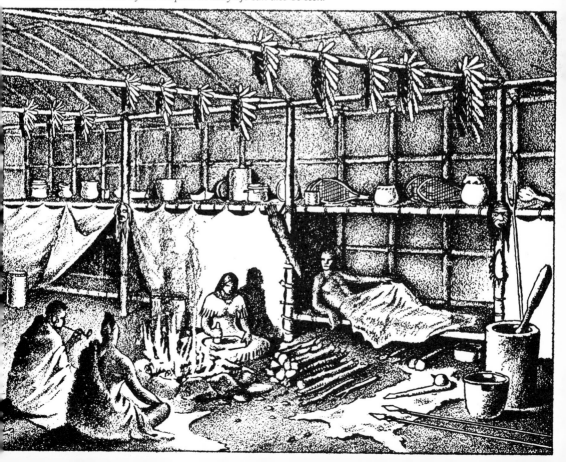

Iroquois cradle board similar to the one Hiawatha may have been placed in as a baby.

were so important to the Iroquois that they called themselves the *Hodenosaunee,* meaning "People of the Longhouse." A typical Iroquois village contained about ten longhouses, each of which was home to about ten families, most of them related. Each family's section of the longhouse was screened off from the others by animal skins.

If Hiawatha was a typical baby, his mother carried him around on her back in a wooden cradle board. While doing her farm work or washing clothes in the stream, she hung the board, with Hiawatha in it, from a tree branch. This allowed her to keep an eye on her baby as the breeze swayed him to sleep. Little Hiawatha wore diapers made of moss and played with a bark rattle that had small stones inside.

Turtle-shell rattles such as this were used in Iroquois religious ceremonies. Hiawatha's rattle would have been simpler and made of folded hickory bark.

Hiawatha's mother probably did the bulk of the family's farming and cooking in addition to most of the child rearing. Because the Iroquois felt that females had better judgment than males, she would also have been involved in making her people's major decisions. The oldest woman in each longhouse was in charge of everyone in it. The women chose the leaders, known in English as *chiefs,* told them what to say at tribal meetings, and decided when the men should go to war.

Hiawatha's father and his uncles on his mother's side were responsible for providing meat for the family. The men hunted deer, bears, and wild turkeys with bows and arrows and spears. They used bone hooks and nets made of plant fiber to fish in their homeland's crystal-blue lakes and rivers. The men also did the fighting in time of war.

The elders in Hiawatha's family would have been considered very important people, too. Since the Iroquois had no written language as yet, they depended on the older people to hand down tribal beliefs and values to the children. As his family sat around the fire on winter nights, Hiawatha listened while the elders spoke of the many spirits that lived in the woods, waters, and sky. He was taught to pray to the spirit of the stream before crossing it, and to the spirit of the forest before entering it.

An Iroquois chief photographed about one hundred years ago.
Hiawatha's grandfather may have looked like this.

Dancing was part of Iroquois religious ceremonies. This painting is The Seneca Eagle Dance by Iroquois artist Ernest Smith.

Hiawatha also must have learned about the important twin spirits known as Teharonhiawagon, or the Creator, and Tawiskaron, or the Evil Mind. The Evil Mind had fashioned much of what was bad in the world, including poisonous plants, the monstrous man-beings without bodies known as the Flying Heads, and the hatred that breeds in the human heart. The Creator had made the first people out of lumps of wet clay. It was believed that, after death, people who had followed the

An Iroquois warrior, as shown in a book published in France in 1796.

right path in life went to live with the Creator in the Sky World, where strawberries grew as large as apples and where flowers of white light were forever in bloom.

The Iroquois did not just eat corn. This mask, which was worn
in religious ceremonies, is made of dried corn husks.

OPPOSITE:
Painting by Iroquois artist John Fadden showing the struggle
between the Creator and his twin, the Evil Mind, at the time of creation.
The Creator is darker and is holding the antlers.

The elders would have explained to Hiawatha what taking "the right path" meant. For one thing, it meant that he must treat his friends and relatives and even passing strangers with kindness. But it also meant that he must treat enemies with all the cruelty that the Evil Mind had hidden in the human heart.

When Hiawatha was a child, there was almost continual fighting among the Iroquois, largely because of a custom known in English as "blood-revenge." Whenever someone was murdered, the victim's male relatives were supposed to kill the murderer. If the murderer had disappeared, a person in his family or village could be killed in his place. "Evening the score" often meant that an innocent person was slain. But the score wouldn't be "even" for long, because soon the new victim's family would take revenge. The result was a steady stream of killings and wars between the Iroquois tribes and villages. Like many generations of Iroquois children before him, Hiawatha undoubtedly was taught that he, too, might have to kill in revenge one day.

By the age of five or six, Hiawatha began doing little tasks to help his family. He chased birds away from the Three Sisters— the corn, beans, and squash that were the Iroquois' most important crops. He also gathered berries and collected maple sap to help feed his family. Collecting maple sap had a very tasty reward. Iroquois children loved "snow food," a delicious treat that was made by pouring hot maple sap over popcorn.

By the age of ten, Iroquois boys began spending more time with their uncles, who were their teachers. Hiawatha's uncles made a small bow and arrow for him, then took him hunting. They also taught him to paddle a canoe out to the best fishing waters. Under his uncles' direction, Hiawatha entered the arrow-shooting contests, races, and wrestling matches that were held for Iroquois boys. These sports were highly competitive, and helped prepare boys to become warriors. Hiawatha probably also played a favorite Indian sport in which two teams used sticks to propel a deerskin ball toward each other's goal. This forerunner of the game of lacrosse was so rough that it was known as "little brother to war."

Two lacrosse sticks used long ago. The larger stick was used by the Iroquois, and the smaller by a tribe from the Maine-New Brunswick (Canada) region.

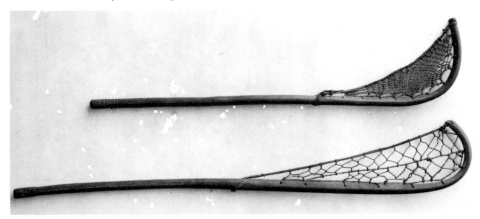

The Hunter, *a painting by the Iroquois artist Ernest Smith.*

Lacrosse Game, *a painting by Ernest Smith showing "little brother to war" in action.*

When he reached manhood, Hiawatha married a woman whose name is lost to history. The couple may have been nearly strangers at the time of their marriage, which was probably arranged by older female relatives. Their wedding ceremony would have been simple. Hiawatha and his wife-to-be exchanged gifts of food, and then the older women on both sides announced that the two young people were married. Hiawatha moved into his wife's longhouse, where they were given their own section. According to various accounts, Hiawatha and his wife had either seven or three daughters.

Hiawatha became a leader of his people—perhaps even a chief. He won fame as an outstanding speaker, but his ideas shocked many of his listeners. To a people who were often at war, Hiawatha spoke of peace. To a people who often seemed to live for revenge, he spoke of friendship among the tribes.

In Hiawatha's time there lived among the Onondaga Indians an evil man named Ododarhoh. Ododarhoh was almost certainly a real man, but in the telling of the Hiawatha story his wickedness has become so exaggerated that he seems almost like the Evil Mind. It is said that Ododarhoh ate people and that his thoughts were so evil they grew out of his head in the form of snakes. The Mohawks even claim that Ododarhoh's fingers were snake heads. Instead of living in a longhouse, Ododarhoh slept on a bed of plants in a marsh. The Onondagas say that Ododarhoh never showed his horrid face except to kill, and that he was known to murder passersby just for talking too loud.

For some reason perhaps linked to the blood-revenge custom, Ododarhoh committed an unspeakably horrible deed. He killed Hiawatha's wife and all of his daughters. The grieving Hiawatha threw himself upon the ground as if he were being tortured. So great was his sorrow that people were afraid to approach and console him.

Hiawatha was expected to kill Ododarhoh in revenge, but this was not in his nature. Killing Ododarhoh would not bring back his wife or daughters. It would only lead to the murder of many more innocent people. Hiawatha was tired of killing, but he was also tired of human beings. He decided to leave the longhouse where he had lived with his wife and daughters. He built a lodge of hemlock branches, and there he lived, alone in the forest.

For some time—exactly how long is unknown—Hiawatha lived as a hermit. He rarely spoke, and people who saw him moving sadly through the forest avoided him. Then one day a man stopped at Hiawatha's lodge. This man, whose name was Degandawida but whom the Iroquois call the Peacemaker, was said to belong to the Hurons, a Canadian tribe related to the

*Sculpture by Iroquois artist Cleveland Sandy, showing
the evil Ododarhoh's snake-covered head.*

The Iroquois artist John Fadden's painting showing the grief of Hiawatha.

Iroquois. He was a kind of preacher, and he was trying to spread a strange idea among the Iroquois people. The five Iroquois tribes and the tribes related to them should stop fighting each other and join together in peace, he preached. But the Peacemaker was finding it difficult to convince the Iroquois to do this. For one thing, he was an outsider. He also stuttered and could not get the words he wanted to say out of his mouth easily.

As the Peacemaker stammered out his ideas, Hiawatha felt himself returning to the world of the living. He realized that this man's views and his own were the same. It was too late to help his own family, but perhaps he and the Peacemaker working together could save many other lives.

The two men made a plan. The five Iroquois tribes would form a government in which each tribe would be represented. This government would settle disputes among the Iroquois and determine when the five tribes would fight a common enemy. The blood-revenge custom was to end. Murderers would pay a price for their crimes instead of being killed. The Iroquois used strings of white and purple shells, called *wampum,* as decorations. A murderer would pay the victim's family a certain number of strings of wampum. Hiawatha and the Peacemaker knew that a price couldn't be set on a human life, but they felt that this arrangement was better than an endless number of murders.

Hiawatha left his lonely lodge, and began traveling with the Peacemaker from village to village. People now listened to Hiawatha, and not just because he spoke well. If a man whose wife and children had been murdered could forsake revenge, then perhaps there was meaning to his words. The idea of a national Iroquois government was also appealing. It would help the Iroquois settle their own conflicts and strengthen them against their common enemies.

The two men convinced most of the Iroquois to join into a federation, but there was one great stumbling block. The Onondagas would not join the federation because Hiawatha's great enemy, Ododarhoh, made it known that he objected to the idea. The thought of speaking to the murderer of his family sickened Hiawatha, yet he knew that the federation would fail unless all five tribes belonged.

Hiawatha struggled with himself for a long time. Finally, he made a decision. He would speak to Ododarhoh for the sake of his people—those of his own time and those to come. It is said that the Peacemaker went with Hiawatha to the marsh where Ododarhoh lived and that Hiawatha soothed the monster by

singing to him. Hiawatha then spoke the message of peace to Ododarhoh—or rather to the hissing snakes atop his head, as the story was told. When Hiawatha finished speaking of peace and Iroquois unity, Ododarhoh raised his head. Hiawatha and the Peacemaker prepared to die, but Ododarhoh did not attack. Instead, he said that he would change his ways and live by their teachings. According to legend, Hiawatha then combed the snakes out of Ododarhoh's hair. Many Iroquois claim that this was the moment when this messenger of peace was given the name *Hiawatha,* which may mean "He Who Combs."

Ododarhoh led the Onondagas into the Iroquois Federation, and soon some Senecas who were the last remaining holdouts also joined. This marked the birth of a new way of life for the People of the Longhouse. An Onondaga town near present-day Syracuse, New York, was made the Iroquois capital. A special longhouse was built there as the capitol building. The women elected about ten chiefs from each tribe as delegates to the national government, which was later known in English as the Grand Council.

Hiawatha and the Peacemaker created a constitution, or set of laws, for the Iroquois. One law stated that the delegates had to meet at least once every few years. They would meet more often when emergencies arose or when one of the tribes needed to

Ernest Smith's 1936 painting showing Hiawatha (seated)
and the Peacemaker (standing) talking to Ododarhoh.

discuss something. Each member of the Grand Council would wear a pair of deer antlers as a symbol of his place in the national government.

It is also said that around this time the Peacemaker chose the pine tree as a symbol of peace between the five Iroquois tribes and that Hiawatha invented a way to record important events. Hiawatha took large numbers of purple and white wampum beads and used them to make pictures that told a story. The Iroquois then began to record their major events on wampum belts in picture form. Some of these belts are now in museums, but they are not our main sources of information about Hiawatha. Our primary sources are the stories that the Iroquois elders have handed down to their young people for generations.

Little is known about Hiawatha's remaining years. The Mohawks claim that he spent his last years clearing rocks from rivers to make it easier for the Iroquois to visit each others' villages. Another widespread belief is that, once their life's work was complete, Hiawatha and the Peacemaker canoed across two different lakes in the New York region and disappeared into the setting sun. It is said that the two of them had found a new road, the path of the peacemaker, to the Sky World. The spirits of both men are said to dwell there happily, where strawberries are as large as apples and where flowers of white light are forever in bloom.

After the deaths of Hiawatha and the Peacemaker, the Iroquois Federation grew stronger. In fact, the Iroquois became the most powerful American Indians north of Mexico. This was good for tribes whom the Iroquois took under their wings, but disastrous for those whom they conquered.

The Iroquois Federation flourished for about three hundred years, until the Revolutionary War (1775–1783). The People of the Longhouse disagreed on whether to support the Americans or the English during this war. In the end, most of them sided with the English because they felt that the Americans wanted all of their lands. In 1779, to punish some Iroquois for raiding American settlements, United States soldiers slaughtered Iroquois families and burned Iroquois towns. These events marked the end of the Iroquois Federation as a powerful force and caused the People of the Longhouse to scatter. Yet to this day some of the 80,000 Iroquois who live in Canada, New York State, Wisconsin, and elsewhere send delegates to the Grand Council that still meets periodically at the old Iroquois capital near Syracuse, New York. And, although few people know it, many historians claim that all Americans live according to some of Hiawatha's and the Peacemaker's ideas.

*This painting by Iroquois artist Arnold Jacobs shows
the tree of peace on the back of a turtle, which
represents the world.*

The Hiawatha Wampum Belt, which dates from about the year 1650, commemorates the founding of the Iroquois Federation by Hiawatha and the Peacemaker. The tree of peace is connected to the rectangles, which represent the Iroquois people.

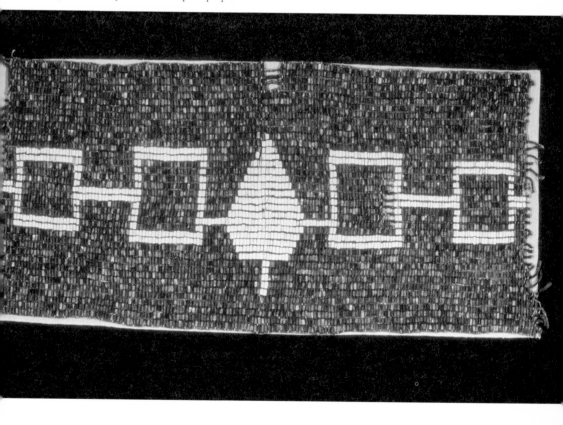

In 1787 American leaders created the United States Constitution, the nation's basic laws. Several of the Founding Fathers who helped create the Constitution knew about the Iroquois Federation and apparently borrowed ideas from it for the United States government. For example, each state sends senators and representatives to Washington, D.C., just as each Iroquois tribe sent delegates to their capital. And each state retains certain powers, just as each Iroquois tribe retained certain powers despite being part of the Federation. In this way, the teachings of two little-known men who lived so long ago have become a basic part of life for all Americans.

BIBLIOGRAPHY

Fenton, William N., ed. *Parker on the Iroquois*. Syracuse, NY: Syracuse University Press, 1968.

Graymont, Barbara. *The Iroquois*. New York: Chelsea House, 1988.

Gridley, Marion E. *The Story of the Iroquois*. New York: Putnam, 1969.

Hale, Horatio, ed. *The Iroquois Book of Rites*. Philadelphia: D. G. Brinton, 1893.

Henry, Thomas R. *Wilderness Messiah: The Story of Hiawatha and the Iroquois*. New York: William Sloane Associates, 1955.

Hewitt, J. N. B. *Iroquoian Cosmology*. New York: AMS Press, 1974.

Longfellow, Henry Wadsworth. *The Song of Hiawatha*. New York: Duell, Sloan and Pearce, 1966.

Schoolcraft, Henry R. *The Myth of Hiawatha*. Millwood, NY: Kraus Reprint Co., 1977.

INDEX

PICTURE CREDITS

p. 2   *Ironwood (Michigan) Area Chamber of Commerce*
p. 4   *Historical Pictures Service, Chicago*
p. 6   *Library of Congress*
p. 7   *Tom Dunnington*
p. 8   *Historical Pictures Service, Chicago*
p. 9   *Historical Pictures Service, Chicago*
p. 10   *Smithsonian Institution*
p. 11   *Smithsonian Institution*
p. 12   *Smithsonian Institution*
p. 14   *Smithsonian Institution*
p. 15   *Library of Congress*
p. 16   *Iroquois Indian Museum, Schoharie, New York*
p. 17   *Smithsonian Institution*
p. 19   *Smithsonian Institution*
p. 20   *From the Ernest Smith Collection, Rochester Museum & Science Center, Rochester, New York*
p. 21   *From the Ernest Smith Collection, Rochester Museum & Science Center, Rochester, New York*
p. 24   *Iroquois Indian Museum, Schoharie, New York*
p. 25   *Iroquois Indian Museum, Schoharie, New York*
p. 28   *From the Ernest Smith Collection, Rochester Museum & Science Center, Rochester, New York*
p. 32   *Iroquois Indian Museum, Schoharie, New York*
p. 33   *Courtesy of the New York State Museum*

Dennis Brindell Fradin

grew up in Chicago, Illinois, and earned a B.A. in creative writing from Northwestern University. He was an elementary school teacher for twelve years and is the author of over one hundred nonfiction books, ranging in subject from the fifty states to medicine and astronomy. In 1989, Dennis Fradin was honored as an Outstanding Contributor to Education by the National College of Education in Evanston, Illinois. His special interests include astronomy and baseball.

Dennis Fradin is married and has three children. His wife, Judith Bloom Fradin, worked with him in obtaining the pictures for *Hiawatha: Messenger of Peace*. They currently live in Evanston, Illinois.